The Mystery of the Haunted Lighthouse

Elspeth Campbell Murphy
Illustrated by Joe Nordstrom

BETHANY HOUSE PUBLISHERS
MINNEAPOLIS, MINNESOTA 55438

Cover and story illustrations by Joe Nordstrom

Three Cousins Detective Club is a trademark
of Elspeth Campbell Murphy.

Published by Bethany House Publishers
A Ministry of Bethany Fellowship, Inc.
11300 Hampshire Avenue South
Minneapolis, Minnesota 55438

Printed in the United States of America.

Library of Congress Cataloging-in-Publication Data

CIP applied for

ISBN 1–55661–411–X   CIP

In loving memory of my father-in-law,
Howard R. Murphy,
whose life was filled with
love, joy, peace,
patience, kindness, goodness,
faithfulness, gentleness, and self-control.

ELSPETH CAMPBELL MURPHY has been a familiar name in Christian publishing for over fifteen years, with more than seventy-five books to her credit and sales reaching five million worldwide. She is the author of the best-selling series *David and I Talk to God* and *The Kids From Apple Street Church*, as well as the 1990 Gold Medallion winner *Do You See Me, God?* A graduate of Trinity College and Moody Bible Institute, Elspeth and her husband, Mike, make their home in Chicago, where she writes full time.

Contents

THE THREE COUSINS
DETECTIVE CLUB

———————

1

A Mysterious Note

*I*f Sarah-Jane Cooper had known that the lighthouse was haunted, she wouldn't have wanted to go there on vacation.

Not that she would have had much choice, of course. Parents were the ones who made vacation plans. But Sarah-Jane could kick up quite a fuss when she needed to. So her parents might have listened to her. Or they might have told her not to let her imagination run away with her.

Who knew?

Certainly none of them knew at the beginning about the lighthouse being haunted.

Not Sarah-Jane.

Not her parents.

Not her cousins Timothy Dawson and

Titus McKay, who were visiting when the note came.

It had all started with the arrival of that note. But the note hadn't said anything about ghosts. In fact, it hadn't said much of anything at all.

When her father opened the envelope, a snapshot fell out. That was all.

The snapshot showed a beautiful, old lighthouse. It looked kind of lonely and run-down and sad. But it didn't look spooky. Not the least bit.

On the back of the snapshot was a note that said:

Please come stop me before I do something stupid.

The note was followed by a phone number. That was all.

Timothy, Titus, and Sarah-Jane looked at one another. They had a detective club, and they were always on the lookout for mysteries. It sure seemed that they had found one. Or rather, that a mystery had found them.

Then, to their great surprise, Sarah-Jane's parents burst out laughing.

2

Ned and Mr. Bo-Bo

"**N**ed!" exclaimed Sarah-Jane's parents together. They hurried to call the number on the back of the snapshot.

Timothy and Titus turned to Sarah-Jane. "Who's Ned?" asked Timothy.

"And what stupid thing is he going to do?" asked Titus.

Sarah-Jane shrugged. "Beats me."

Her parents talked to Ned for what seemed like ages. When they finally got off the phone, Sarah-Jane could tell something was up.

"Who's Ned?" she asked.

"He's an old friend of our family," said her mother. "Though I don't suppose you would remember him. He's the one who gave you Mr. Bo-Bo."

"Ex-*cuse* me?" said Timothy.

"Mr. *Who*?" said Titus.

"Mr. Bo-Bo," said Sarah-Jane with as much dignity as she could muster. "My all-time favorite stuffed animal. When I was little, I used to take him with me everywhere. I still have him. He's sitting on the shelf over my bed. He's the monkey wearing the sailor suit."

"Ah, yes," said Titus, shaking his head sadly. "I've seen that monkey. Mr. Bo-Bo looks as if he's had a hard life."

"He's a wreck," agreed Timothy.

"He is *not* a wreck!" protested Sarah-Jane.

"You *did* drag him around by his tail . . ." said her mother.

"And you *did* chew off his ear . . ." said her father.

"But that doesn't mean Mr. Bo-Bo wasn't happy!" wailed Sarah-Jane.

Everyone laughed. Sarah-Jane had to admit that she was getting carried away. Again.

To change the subject, Sarah-Jane said, "What stupid thing is Ned going to do?"

"Oh, nothing much," said Sarah-Jane's father. "He just wants to buy a lighthouse."

3

An Educational Vacation

*S*arah-Jane held up the snapshot. (She liked it so much her parents said she could have it.) She said, "*This* lighthouse? Ned wants to buy *this* lighthouse?"

Her father nodded. "That's the one."

"Neat-O!" said Timothy.

"EXcellent!" said Titus.

"So cool!" said Sarah-Jane.

"Well, hold on now," said her mother. "He hasn't actually bought it yet. He needs to know if it can be fixed up and how much that will cost. That's why he sent us the note. He wants Daddy to look the place over and give him some advice."

The cousins nodded. That made sense. Sarah-Jane's father was a builder. He knew all about these things. And both Art and Sue Cooper *loved* old buildings and all kinds of antiques.

"Does he really want you to talk him out of buying it, Uncle Art?" asked Timothy, thinking of the note.

His uncle laughed. "Not a chance!" Then he said more seriously, "Owning a lighthouse has been Ned's lifelong dream. He's always wanted to open one up as a bed and breakfast. I hope it works out for him—and for the lighthouse. It's important to save these old treasures. We'll know more tomorrow when we see it."

"What!?" cried the cousins together.

"Oh, yes," said Sarah-Jane's father. "Didn't I mention that we're all going up there?"

"Daddy!" said Sarah-Jane. "You *know* you didn't!" (He was always doing this.)

Her father laughed again. (He knew he was always doing this.) "Seriously. It will work out great. We'll take a detour on our way up to the cabin. Get a good look at the lighthouse. It will be very"—he paused dramatically—"Educational!"

The cousins groaned. They should have seen this coming.

Earlier in the year, the three sets of parents had gotten together to plan vacations. They had decided the cousins were old enough—ten—to go on vacation with one another. The parents had also decided the trips should be Educational. With a capital E. So all three cousins were going on all three Educational Vacations.

That's why Timothy and Titus were at Sarah-Jane's house. They were leaving early the next morning with Sarah-Jane and her parents for the cabin at Misty Pines Campground.

The cousins had been together at Misty Pines before. But this year it would be Educational. Nature hikes. Bird watching. And now, it seemed, a lighthouse, too.

Later, in her room, Sarah-Jane looked at Ned's snapshot again.

She had groaned when her father used the word *Educational.* But actually, Sarah-Jane wanted to know all about the lighthouse. She hoped they would be allowed to climb the tower.

Sarah-Jane was not the least bit afraid of

heights. Sarah-Jane was not the least bit afraid of a lot of things. Real things, that is. Like deep water and fast rides.

Where she had a problem was with imaginary things. Like ghosts. Sarah-Jane knew there were no such things as ghosts. But she was afraid of them anyway.

The strange thing was, she actually liked *hearing* ghost stories. It was fun with lots of people around and everyone shivering and squealing.

What Sarah-Jane hated was *remembering*

ghost stories when she was alone in her room in the dark.

Sarah-Jane looked at the picture of the lighthouse again. It looked lonely and run-down and sad. But not the least bit spooky.

She looked again. Well, maybe it was a *little* spooky.

On impulse, she opened her suitcase and shoved in Mr. Bo-Bo. She told herself it was so Ned could see him again.

4

Pancakes and Lighthouses

*T*hey left early the next day. *Extra* early, since they were going to take a detour to see the lighthouse.

As usual, Timothy was wide awake. He was always bright-eyed and bushy-tailed first thing in the morning.

As usual, Titus was hardly awake at all. His aunt and uncle practically had to carry him to the car.

This morning Sarah-Jane was somewhere in between. Groggy. Not as zonked as Titus. But certainly not as zippy as Timothy.

They hadn't gone all that far when Sarah-Jane's father stopped at a pancake house for breakfast. That perked her right up. In Sarah-Jane's opinion, eating breakfast out was one of the absolutely best parts of vacation.

She and Timothy hauled Titus into the restaurant and propped him up in the booth.

When Titus finally woke up, he looked around as if to say: Who am I? Where am I? How did I get here? Who are you people?

But what he actually said was, "I don't get it, Uncle Art. How can somebody *buy* a lighthouse? I mean, aren't they public property or something?"

Sarah-Jane's father beamed with delight and clapped Titus on the shoulder. "I'm glad you asked that, my boy!"

The cousins groaned.

"Thanks a lot, Ti," said Sarah-Jane.

"Yeah. Nice going, Ti," said Timothy.

Titus put his head in his hands and said, "Oh, no! What have I done?"

But nothing could stop Art Cooper now. "No comments from the peanut gallery," he said. "This trip is going to be Educational."

The cousins groaned again. But it was really just for show. They were actually pretty interested. And the grown-ups knew it.

"To answer your question, Titus," said his uncle, "you're right. Lighthouses are government property. These days they're managed by the Coast Guard. Some of them are open for tours. Some of them are part of public parks. But they're not for sale anymore. However, years ago, when lighthouses were being automated, the government didn't need all the old towers. So some were sold to private buyers."

Timothy said, "So if you wanted to buy a lighthouse now, you'd have to get it from someone who had already bought it from the government a long time ago. Right?"

"That's right," said Sarah-Jane's mother. "So, as you can imagine, lighthouses don't come on the market that often. Ned was so excited to hear about this one! The old owner recently died, but his relatives don't want to keep the lighthouse. The nephew who's selling it knows Ned. And he said Ned could have the first chance to buy it. I just hope it all works out OK."

By this time Sarah-Jane was full of pancakes and feeling pretty good. She thought to herself: *Ned wants to buy a lighthouse that's for sale. What can possibly go wrong?*

5

The Lighthouse Keeper

*L*ater on in the car Sarah-Jane thought about what her father had said. He had used a word . . . what was it? She sort of knew what it meant. But she wasn't sure.

"Daddy, what was that word you used about lighthouses? *Automated?* What exactly does automated mean?"

Her father was delighted. "I'm glad you asked that, Sarah-Jane!"

The cousins groaned.

"Thanks a lot, S-J," said Timothy.

"Yeah. Nice going, S-J," said Titus.

Sarah-Jane clapped a hand to her head. "Oh, no!" she cried. "What have I done?"

But she really did want to know what automated meant.

Her father explained that before buildings had electricity, people used to burn oil for light. A light that guided ships had to be up high. So a lighthouse was actually a tower with an oil lamp on top.

That meant someone had to climb the winding staircase every day at sunset to light the oil lamp. And he had to climb back up again at sunrise to put the light out.

But that wasn't all. The lamp was enclosed in a giant glass lantern—a lens—that was shaped like a beehive. The lens reflected the light into a bright beam. Since oil lamps were smoky, the lens had to be kept clean. Otherwise the light wouldn't show through. The same went for the windows.

"It was a lot of work," said Sarah-Jane's mother. "But it had to be done day in and day out. The lighthouse keeper had to be faithful. So many people were depending on him. Or her. Women could be lighthouse keepers, too."

That got Sarah-Jane thinking. Sure it was a lot of work. But you could live in a pretty place near the water. And wasn't her grandmother always bragging about how dependable Sarah-Jane, Timothy, and Titus were?

Sarah-Jane said what she was thinking: "Maybe I'll be a lighthouse keeper one day."

"Oh, sorry, honey!" said her father. "We kind of got away from your question, didn't we? But I'm afraid that's what automated means. It means there are no more lighthouse keepers. Everything is done automatically by electricity now. No one has to climb all those winding stairs to light an oil lamp. There's even a machine to change the light bulbs. New lights have to be checked only once in a while."

Sarah-Jane's father was really getting going. He added, "The bigger ships don't even *need* lighthouses anymore. They find their way by radar. Smaller boats still need the lights, of course. That's why a lot of the old towers now have electric lights in them. But some of the new lights are so small they can just go on top of a pole. That means a lot of the old towers are just standing empty. That's why it's so good when people get together to fix them up to make parks and museums."

It was a favorite subject with Sarah-Jane's father. Faithfully saving old buildings. Making them look the way they had when they were new. That's why Ned had asked for his advice.

Timothy, who wanted to be an artist, said, "Why do they paint lighthouses with stripes and stuff?"

Before Sarah-Jane's father could answer, everyone else said at the same time, "We're glad you asked that, Timothy!"

Sarah-Jane's father pretended to ignore them.

"It's called a daymark, my good boy. Different lighthouses have different shapes and designs. When a captain sees a lighthouse, he can look up the description on his charts. The charts tell him which lighthouse he's looking at. That's how he knows where he is. At night he can tell by the pattern of the flashes."

Sarah-Jane took out Ned's snapshot of the lighthouse and looked at it.

But nothing could have prepared her for the real thing. For how she felt when they finally came to the end of a bumpy road.

And there it was.

6

Ned and Mr. Bo-Bo Again

*T*he cousins got out of the car and looked up. They couldn't help it. A lighthouse does that to people. It was sort of like a steeple on a church, Sarah-Jane thought. It just makes you look up.

A shiver ran along her arms. But it wasn't a scared shiver. It was the excited shiver you get from seeing something grand.

It seemed her cousins felt the same way.

"EXcellent!" said Titus.

"Neat-O!" said Timothy.

"So cool!" agreed Sarah-Jane.

She was glad to see that the lighthouse didn't look spooky after all. It looked lonely

24

and run-down and sad. But at the same time, it looked so peaceful and beautiful in the sunshine that played among the clouds.

Of course, that was just it, Sarah-Jane reminded herself. Just about any place looked good in the sunshine. But what if it were nighttime? Or even a gray, dreary afternoon?

Suddenly a gust of wind blew off the water, and Sarah-Jane shivered again. But this time she couldn't tell if she was scared or just cold.

Either way, she didn't have time to think about it, because just then a car pulled up.

Out jumped a man about her parents' age. He had sandy red hair, freckles, and one of the nicest smiles Sarah-Jane had ever seen.

This had to be Ned. Sarah-Jane liked him at once.

"You got here!" Ned cried. He made it sound as if they had walked all the way and that they were the most wonderful people on earth to do this for him. Sarah-Jane didn't know when she had ever felt more welcome.

It turned out Ned had once visited the Coopers when Timothy and Titus were also there. But he hadn't seen any of the cousins since they were very small. So he kept saying they couldn't be—they just *couldn't* be—Timothy, Titus, and Sarah-Jane.

Sarah-Jane had noticed that adults always thought kids grew up so fast. But she didn't think kids grew up fast at all. She thought it took forever.

"So what am I saying?" Ned wondered aloud. "That Art and Sue Cooper left the babies at home? That they hired three look-alike ten-year-olds to come make me feel old? No, you kids probably are who you say you are."

"I don't know about these boys," said Sarah-Jane. "I never saw them before in my life. But at least I have proof about me!"

She pushed the button to open the trunk so that she could dig around in her suitcase. She found what she was looking for and held him up high. "Taa-daa!"

"Well, as I live and breathe!" cried Ned. "It's Mr. Bo-Bo! How sweet of you to bring him to show me, Sarah-Jane! Good old Mr. Bo-Bo. He hasn't changed a bit."

Titus said with a straight face, "You mean he looked like that when you bought him? You sure pick out nice presents."

"Why, thank you," said Ned, trying to keep

a straight face, too. "I didn't want our little Sarah-Jane to have to break him in."

"Well, somebody sure broke him in," said Timothy. "He's a wreck."

"He is *not* a wreck!" wailed Sarah-Jane.

"And speaking of wrecks," said Ned, with a sweep of his arm. "What do you think of my lighthouse? It's seen better days. . . ."

"Like a certain monkey I could name," said Timothy.

Sarah-Jane covered up Mr. Bo-Bo's one good ear so he wouldn't get his feelings hurt.

"Well, I won't know until I take a closer look," said Sarah-Jane's father. "But my guess is that this lighthouse will see good days again. It's just that . . . well, there's something odd here."

7

Something Odd Here

"Odd in what way?" asked Ned.

"Well, it's the craziest thing," replied Sarah-Jane's father. "From what I've seen so far, the place is in great shape. The building looks solid. It's been well cared for. But there's all this surface damage."

Ned asked, "So you're saying the lighthouse *looks* to be in worse shape than it really is?"

"Exactly," said Sarah-Jane's father. "And that's not unusual. A broken shutter or chipped paint can make even a solid building look bad. The odd part is that this damage wasn't done by time or the wind and the rain. This damage was done on purpose. And not too long ago, either."

"Vandals?" cried Ned.

Sarah-Jane's father sighed. "It sure looks like it."

"What makes somebody do something like that?" exclaimed Sarah-Jane's mother.

They were all quiet, wondering about it.

Then Timothy said slowly, "You know, for vandals, they sure didn't do a very good job."

Everyone looked at him in surprise.

Timothy hurried to explain. "What I mean is . . . well, there's this school near me. Not the one I go to, but it's in my district. Anyway, last year a couple of kids broke into it—and they just went crazy! I mean, they really *trashed* the place. The police caught the guys who did it. But I heard it took like a hundred thousand dollars to get the place back to normal."

Titus, who lived in a big city, nodded his agreement. "And there's no spray paint here, either. The first thing kids do if they want to mess up a place is spray-paint it."

"Right," said Sarah-Jane. "Or throw eggs at it. I don't see any egg mess. And there's no broken glass, either. Usually if one window gets broken and nobody fixes it, pretty soon all the windows get broken. The kids figure it doesn't matter if they throw rocks there."

The grown-ups stared at them in amazement. "How do you *know* all this stuff?" they asked.

The cousins shrugged. Even if you were a good kid who hardly ever got in trouble, you still heard about things. You still knew what was going on.

Titus summed it up. "So what we're saying is: Why didn't the vandals trash the place? Why did they just do small stuff here and there?"

Sarah-Jane said, "Maybe they liked the lighthouse. Maybe they didn't really want to hurt it."

"Then why do anything at all?" asked Timothy.

Sarah-Jane looked up at the lighthouse again. Dark, heavy clouds were gathering in the sky.

8

It's a Mystery

Sarah-Jane was glad when Ned suggested lunch first and a tour of the lighthouse later. She told herself it had nothing to do with the vandalism or the darkening sky. It was just that it had been a long time since breakfast. And, in Sarah-Jane's opinion, eating lunch out was second only to eating breakfast out.

"There's a little town only a couple of miles away," Ned told them. "That's good if I'm going to open a bed and breakfast. A lot of lighthouses are just too far away from anything else. Some you can't get to except by boat. There's a little diner in town here. Nothing fancy. But the food is *great*! My treat."

Timothy, Titus, and Sarah-Jane all wanted to ride with Ned. When the grown-ups said

OK, the three cousins raced to Ned's car.

Timothy and Titus didn't even try for the front seat. They liked Ned, of course. And he liked them. But it was just sort of understood among the cousins that the boys were relatives of the main friend.

So Sarah-Jane got the front seat.

Ned was still holding Mr. Bo-Bo, so the monkey got to ride up front, too. Sarah-Jane propped him up on the dashboard, being careful to turn him so that he could see out. *Really*, she told herself sternly. *I have got to stop letting my imagination run away with me. He's just a stuffed animal. Aren't you, Mr. Bo-Bo?*

She thought again about the lighthouse. She asked Ned, "Will the man—the old owner's nephew—have to fix up the place to sell it?"

"It depends on what we work out," Ned told her. "I might decide to buy it 'as is.' He's promised I could have first chance. And he's been good about letting me have the key."

Sarah-Jane had a sudden thought. "You don't suppose he changed his mind, do you? Maybe he wants to keep it after all. But he already promised you that you could buy it. So—maybe he messed it up to make *you* change your mind?"

As soon as she had said that, Sarah-Jane wondered if it sounded too farfetched. Was her imagination working overtime again?

Honestly, she told herself. *It's getting so I can't tell a good idea from a crazy one.* Except Sarah-Jane knew from experience that sometimes crazy ideas turned out to be splendid. And sometimes crazy ideas turned out to be . . . crazy ideas.

Ned took her seriously. "I see what you're saying, Sarah-Jane. And if I didn't know this guy, I'd say you could be right. But I'm sure he really wants to sell. So I don't know *what's* going on. I love the lighthouse. But I'm concerned about who did the damage and why."

Sarah-Jane felt sorry for Ned. She knew from experience that it was confusing to be excited about something and worried about it all at the same time.

Ned sighed. "It's a mystery to me."

"Well, then," said Titus. "You need the T.C.D.C."

9

The T.C.D.C.

"What's a 'teesy-deesy'?" asked Ned.

"It's letters," explained Sarah-Jane. "Capital T. Capital C. Capital D. Capital C. It stands for the Three Cousins Detective Club."

"And that's you three?" asked Ned.

"That's us," said Timothy.

"And you've actually solved some mysteries?" asked Ned. He sounded impressed.

The cousins looked at one another and grinned. "A few."

By this time they had reached the restaurant. Sarah-Jane's parents had stopped off along the road to take some pictures. So Ned and the cousins went inside to wait for them.

They waited in the little entryway between the outer door and the inner door.

35

The entryway had a newspaper stand and a candy machine. So it got pretty crowded when the four of them came in.

There was already someone there with his back to them. A teenage boy stood studying the candy bar choices in the vending machine. He seemed to make a big point of ignoring a grown-up and three "little" kids.

Sarah-Jane didn't care. She knew some of her friends would think he was cute. But she thought teenagers who went around trying to look bored out of their minds just looked dumb.

Timothy and Titus were still talking about the weird damage at the lighthouse. Ned was saying that maybe the cousins could scout around for clues after lunch. And Timothy and Titus were all for it.

Sarah-Jane tried not to gulp. Sure, she wanted to help Ned. But she wondered what the T.C.D.C. had gotten themselves into.

Suddenly she heard herself saying, "I'm just glad the lighthouse isn't haunted, Ned."

She hadn't meant to bring the subject up. The words had just popped out.

But she was even more surprised to hear

Ned say, "Me, too! Lighthouses have more than their share of ghost stories. But I haven't heard any stories about this one. It's a good thing, too. Someone with my overactive imagination shouldn't buy a haunted house."

As soon as Ned said "overactive imagination," Timothy and Titus pointed at Sarah-Jane.

Sarah-Jane tried to look blank. "What?"

Ned laughed at the boys. "Now, don't you give my girl a hard time. She's just like me. Aren't you, Sarah-Jane? We know there are no such things as ghosts. But they still give us the willies."

At that moment, the teenage boy finally made a decision. He yanked on a handle, and the candy machine clanked. Sarah-Jane jumped. The boy had been so quiet, she had forgotten he was even there. The sudden noise startled her.

The boy caught her eye. He smiled to himself as if it were funny the way she had jumped. Then he strolled outside, hopped on his bike, and rode off.

Sarah-Jane expressed an opinion: "What a jerk!"

10

Cobwebs

*N*ed was right about the food at the diner. It was great. As they headed back to the lighthouse, the sky was dark and gloomy. But at least it looked as if the rain would hold off. That was good—the lighthouse would look too scary in a storm. But now that Sarah-Jane knew the lighthouse wasn't haunted, she was looking forward to going inside. Sort of.

As they pulled up to the lighthouse, Sarah-Jane took Mr. Bo-Bo off the dashboard. She didn't exactly want to carry him around. But she didn't exactly want to pack him away again, either. In the end, she decided to set him on the hood of their own car. That way she could still see him. Besides, Mr. Bo-Bo liked to sit outside whenever he got the chance.

The house was bigger than she had expected. It was actually a double house. One side had been for the lighthouse keeper and his family. The other side had been for the lighthouse keeper's assistant.

There would be plenty of room for the bed and breakfast Ned was so excited about opening. The three grown-ups were chattering away about knocking down this wall and adding that one.

Sarah-Jane was just relieved to see there weren't any cobwebs. It wasn't that Sarah-Jane was afraid of spiders. She wasn't. It's just that cobwebs always made a house look spooky.

Sarah-Jane lived in an old house herself. And last summer, before her father had put in new windows, the spiders were always getting in. You had to clean away cobwebs from the corners of the ceiling almost every day. . . .

"That's funny," she said softly.

"Funny ha-ha? Or funny weird?" asked Timothy.

"Funny weird."

"What's funny weird?" asked Titus.

"That there aren't any cobwebs," said Sarah-Jane. She explained to her cousins about the spiders. "So why *wouldn't* there be any cobwebs?" she asked them.

"I see what you're saying," said Titus. "Someone may have messed up the outside of the house. But the inside is neat and clean."

"Too clean?" asked Timothy.

"Exactly," said Sarah-Jane. She shivered. It would have been less spooky to see cobwebs.

11

A Light in the Darkness

"*A*nd wait till you see this!" cried Ned.

The cousins put aside the question of the cobwebs and went to join the grown-ups at the back door.

"Come on out into the yard, everybody," Ned said. "Sue, you're just going to love this! A genuine antique. And the seller says it goes with the house."

Hung up on a frame in the yard was a big, beautiful bell. It looked old. Very old.

"I think the old owner must have been in the process of restoring it," Ned explained. "Ordinarily a bell like this would hang on the outside of a triangle-shaped building. Inside the building there would be a machine to keep

41

the bell ringing so you wouldn't have to do it by hand."

"Why would you have to keep the bell ringing?" asked Titus. Sarah-Jane and Timothy waited for him to answer his own question. He did that a lot. It was his way of thinking out loud. And his cousins knew that about him. It just so happened they came up with the answer at the exact moment Titus did.

All together they yelled, "FOG!"

"Wow, these are smart kids," said Ned. "Yes, you're exactly right. When boats can't see the light, they have to rely on sound. Hearing something in the fog is tricky, even now. Nowadays, places that get a lot of fog use foghorns.

"But it's good to keep things like this bell from the past. I'd love to have a little museum here. I want to help people understand how the people who went before us lived. Families could come here. And it would be so—"

"Educational?" asked Titus.

"Exactly!" cried Ned.

"Well," said Timothy innocently. "In the interests of education, I think we should ring the bell."

Sarah-Jane was glad that Timothy had said something. She was itching to pull on the rope.

They each got a turn to ring it. It sounded deep and rich and full. But pulling the rope was hard work. Sarah-Jane was glad she didn't have to pull it hour after hour until a heavy fog lifted.

Thinking of fog made her think of spookiness again. Some things about the lighthouse were so cool. And yet . . . there were all these questions. She felt like a bell herself, the way she kept going back and forth about it.

Ned had saved the best till last.

He unlocked the little door at the base of the tower and pulled it open.

Sarah-Jane's father said the stairs were safe to climb and that the cousins could go up by themselves. (It was more of an adventure that way.)

So the cousins got to go up the winding stairway. The steps were narrow, shaped like pieces of pie.

Round and round. Up and up. It was enough to make you dizzy—even if you weren't afraid of heights.

Finally they reached the lantern room at

the very top. (They noticed the windows were sparkling clean.)

And the view was spectacular!

They could see for miles. They could see the tiny town where they had eaten lunch. They could see the new lighthouse farther up the beach. It wasn't a lighthouse, exactly. It was just a plastic light on top of a skinny pole. And it worked just fine.

But it wasn't the same thing, Sarah-Jane thought. She looked out at the water. She imagined what it would be like to be out there in a little boat. At night. With blackness all around you. Black water. Black sky. Not knowing where you were.

And then to look up and see a light shining in the darkness. And to know there was another *person* there. A person who faithfully climbed those winding stairs every night to light the lamp that kept other people safe. A person you could count on. Even if you didn't know him.

She thought about all those people Ned was talking about. The ones who had gone before.

She thought about Ned. And how he had

sent her a present when she was just a baby—long before she even knew him.

She thought about good old Mr. Bo-Bo, waiting for her down below.

She thought—as long as Timothy and Titus weren't looking—that it would be fun to wave to Mr. Bo-Bo.

She crossed to the other side of the lantern room and looked down at the cars.

Mr. Bo-Bo was gone.

12

Missing Monkey

"*H*e's *gone!*" cried Sarah-Jane.

"Who's gone?" asked Timothy.

"Mr. Bo-Bo!"

"Mr. Bo-Bo?" asked Titus. "How could he be gone? The last time I saw him he was on the dashboard of Ned's car."

"I moved him," said Sarah-Jane. She could hear her voice rising. "I put him on the hood of *our* car. And now he's gone!"

"Whoa," said Timothy. "Get a grip, S-J! Maybe you meant to put him on the hood. But maybe you changed your mind and put him somewhere else."

"Yeah, calm down, S-J," said Titus. "Or maybe your mom took him inside the house in case it rained. That's all."

In Sarah-Jane's opinion, when you were all upset, there was nothing worse than someone telling you to calm down. It made you just want to scream.

But she knew her cousins were only trying to help. So she made herself take a deep breath. She agreed to go down and check with her parents. But she knew—she just knew— that they hadn't moved Mr. Bo-Bo.

And she was right.

Her parents were completely wrapped up in Ned's plans for the lighthouse. So they just said things like: You must have mislaid him. He couldn't just walk away. I'm sure he'll turn up. Go look around.

Sarah-Jane knew she could kick up quite a fuss. And that it would get her parents' attention. But what good would it do? They didn't know where Mr. Bo-Bo was. And it wasn't as if she had never mislaid anything before. She had—lots of times. She knew absolutely, positively, though, that she hadn't mislaid Mr. Bo-Bo. But the answer was still the same: Go and look for him.

Timothy and Titus volunteered to help her. Part of being a detective was knowing how to search. And the cousins were very good detectives.

But Mr. Bo-Bo was nowhere to be found.

"You were right, S-J," said Titus at last. "There's something strange going on."

"And it's giving me the creeps," said Timothy.

Sarah-Jane was glad they were all on the same wavelength again.

But that didn't bring Mr. Bo-Bo back.

Part of being a detective was knowing when to stop searching. At least for a while. It helped to take a break. And the cousins were good enough detectives to know that.

Timothy and Titus decided to take a break by looking for something totally different— shells and rocks on the beach.

Sarah-Jane decided to take a break by looking at the sky. It was one of her favorite things to do.

So after the boys went off, Sarah-Jane got the picnic blanket out of the trunk and spread it out on the grass. She needed to be alone for a little while. She needed to tell herself that she hadn't really lost Mr. Bo-Bo.

She lay on her back with her hands behind

her head and looked up at the lighthouse against the sky. The clouds were playing tricks. The way they were moving made it seem as if the lighthouse were moving.

It was fun to watch. Sarah-Jane was just beginning to relax when something about the lantern room caught her eye.

It was a face.

And it was watching her.

13

The Ghost in the Tower

Sarah-Jane didn't scream very often. But when she did, it was enough to wake the dead.

She jumped to her feet and went screaming and scrambling back to the house.

Timothy and Titus came running from the beach.

Her parents and Ned came running from the cellar.

"What is it? What happened?" everyone cried. "You look as if you've seen a ghost!"

"I did! I did! I did see a ghost!" gasped Sarah-Jane. "Up in the tower. This face. Horrible. Ugly. Scary. Face."

"Now, just calm down," said her mother.

Whenever anyone else told her to calm down, it made Sarah-Jane want to scream. But when her mother told her to calm down—gently, firmly—it worked. Sarah-Jane grew quiet.

Her father and Ned went off to check the tower inside and out.

They didn't find anything.

Sarah-Jane never thought they would. Strange things were happening. But it seemed they were happening just to her. First Mr. Bo-Bo. And now this.

"It was probably just the reflection of the clouds on the glass," said her father.

"Reflections and shadows can be pretty scary," said Ned.

Sarah-Jane shrugged. She knew what she had seen. But what good did it do to argue?

"You going to be OK, kiddo?" asked her mother.

Sarah-Jane nodded. Now that the shock had worn off, she was beginning to feel embarrassed.

After making sure she was all right, the grown-ups went back to work in the house.

Timothy and Titus looked at her sympathetically. But Sarah-Jane could tell they didn't know what to say. Who could blame them? She would probably feel the same way if it had happened to one of them.

"Show us where you were when you saw it," suggested Timothy.

So the three of them trooped around to the front of the lighthouse.

"OK," said Titus. "Now tell us again exactly what you saw."

"I saw a face," said Sarah-Jane firmly. "It was big and hideous. Like a monster but still mostly human. You know what I mean? It was like one of those big rubber Halloween masks that fit over your whole head. The really gross kind. Like with green skin and an eyeball hanging out—"

She broke off. A new idea was taking shape in her mind. Maybe it wasn't something unexplainable like a ghost. Maybe it was something explainable, like someone wearing a . . . but that still didn't explain *why.*

She looked at Timothy and Titus. She had a hunch they were thinking the very same thing she was.

But before any of them could say a word, their attention was distracted.

DONG. DONG. DONG. Someone was

ringing the fog bell! Who? The grown-ups?

It didn't seem likely.

They raced around to the back to catch whoever was doing it.

The bell had stopped ringing by the time they got there.

They saw no one.

Except that—

There, with his hand on the rope, sat Mr. Bo-Bo.

14

A Sweet Little Clue

"*H*ey, you three!" yelled Sarah-Jane's father from somewhere inside the house. "Quit messing with that bell! It's a valuable antique."

Sarah-Jane hesitated for a moment. Then she called back, "OK!"

After all that had happened already, what was she supposed to say? *But, Daddy! It wasn't me ringing the bell! It was my stuffed monkey!?* She didn't think so.

And that meant taking the blame for something she didn't do. *Not* her favorite thing at all.

Sarah-Jane stomped over to Mr. Bo-Bo and snatched him up.

She didn't know what was going on. A horrible face in the tower. A ringing bell with no-body there.

But she was sure of one thing: No one was going to lay a finger on Mr. Bo-Bo again.

There was a scrap of paper on the ground. Sarah-Jane swooped down and snatched that up, too. If there was one thing she absolutely, positively could not stand, it was littering.

"S-J," began Timothy.

"*What?*" snapped Sarah-Jane. "What? What? What? What? What?"

"Well, first of all," said Timothy. "You don't sound scared anymore."

"Yes," said Titus. "It's nice to see you're back to your old self again."

"And second of all," said Timothy. "I think you just found a clue. A sweet little clue. I know for a fact it wasn't there before. Because we looked all around here when we were doing our search. And we would have seen it."

Sarah-Jane looked down at the paper in her hand.

It was a piece of candy bar wrapper.

Sarah-Jane grinned. "Do ghosts eat candy bars?"

"No," said Titus. "They like boo-berry

pie. Get it? *Boo*-berry pie?"

Sarah-Jane and Timothy groaned. It was an old, old, *old* one.

"So what do you think?" asked Sarah-Jane. "Do you think it might be that boy from the restaurant?"

"That would be my guess," said Titus. "Even though this 'evidence' wouldn't hold up in court. Anyone could drop a candy wrapper."

Timothy said, "Yeah. But looking back on it, that guy sure took a long time making up his mind at the candy machine. He was in the entryway the whole time we were talking about the vandalism. He was probably listening to every word we said. He knows we didn't fall for the idea that the place is falling apart. He knows Ned still wants to buy it."

"But why should he care what Ned does?" asked Titus.

Sarah-Jane added, "And why pick on me? He heard me say that I was glad the lighthouse wasn't haunted. So he tried to make me think it *was* haunted." She didn't add that the plan had almost worked.

Talking things over was one way the

T.C.D.C. solved mysteries.

But their attention was distracted by a sound again.

This time it was coming from the lighthouse tower. It sounded like chains being dragged up the metal staircase.

Sarah-Jane rolled her eyes. "Oh, give me a break," she said, and went to get something out of the trunk.

Sarah-Jane's mother had a set of sturdy folding chairs she took with them when they traveled. Sarah-Jane got one out and carried it back to the lighthouse door.

There was this trick she had seen on a TV show once. You wedged a chair under the doorknob to keep the doorknob from turning. That way no one could open the door to get in. Or, in *this* case, out.

With the folded chair snugly in place, Timothy and Titus stood guard.

And Sarah-Jane, perfectly calm, went off to get the grown-ups.

15

Out in the Open

*I*t took a while—quite a while—to explain who was pounding on the inside of the door. And why the cousins wouldn't let him out.

But the grown-ups insisted. And the boy, whose name was Jason, was relieved to see them. Even though it turned out he *was* the one who had messed up the lighthouse.

Jason said, "See, the captain—the old man who used to live here—he was like my special friend, you now? And the lighthouse was my special place. So even after he died I'd come over here. I still had the key. And I'd, like, clean up and just hang out. I guess I was lonely or something. I . . . I just didn't want to forget the captain.

"But then I heard that his nephew was going to sell the lighthouse. And I thought, hey, this is *my* lighthouse. Well, I know it isn't really my lighthouse. But, well, you know what I mean. I thought I couldn't stand it if I couldn't come here anymore. So then I thought if the place looked messed up on the outside, people would think it was in bad shape and not want to buy it. I guess that was a dumb idea."

"*Very* dumb!" said Sarah-Jane. "And I DE-MAND to know why you tried to scare me."

She was glad to see that Jason actually took a step back. *Ha!* thought Sarah-Jane. *Who's scared now?*

"That was dumb, too. I admit it. But I know this lighthouse inside out. And I figured I could keep one step ahead of you and not get caught."

Sarah-Jane let that pass. It was obvious to everyone that he *had* gotten caught—and who it was who caught him.

"That still doesn't explain why you picked on me," she said.

"I'm really sorry about that!" said Jason. And he sounded as if he meant it. "But my first plan hadn't worked. I was desperate. I didn't want your dad to buy the lighthouse. I didn't want some little girl twerp—no offense—taking over here. So I thought if you were too scared to live here, your dad wouldn't buy it."

"OK, wait a minute," said Sarah-Jane. "Somebody is seriously mixed-up here. And it's not me. My dad was never going to buy this lighthouse."

"Sure he was," replied Jason. "He was talking about it at the restaurant."

"My dad wasn't even at the restaurant when you were there."

"Sure he was," said Jason. He turned to Ned. "Don't you remember? We were all crowded in that little entryway together."

Suddenly Sarah-Jane understood. She pointed at Ned. "No, no, no! You've got it all wrong. He's my friend. Not my father."

Jason frowned. "Then why did I hear you call him *Dad*?"

Sarah-Jane tried not to roll her eyes, but she couldn't help it. "I didn't call him *Dad*. I called him *Ned*. Ned. Ned. That's his name, NED!"

"Oh," said Jason. He looked so completely clobbered by the "little girl twerp" that everybody laughed.

But Jason cheered up quickly when Ned told him that he would always be welcome at the lighthouse. Beginning with helping Ned to repair the damage.

"And I'd love to hear about your friend the captain," said Ned. "He sounds like an interesting person."

"Oh, he was, sir," said Jason eagerly.

The sun came out just as the cousins were getting ready to leave. The golden rays struck the glass of the lantern room and made it look as if a light still shone there.

"Wow!" said Sarah-Jane's father. "Look at that! Is this a fun vacation, or what?"

The cousins looked at one another and tried not to laugh.

"Yes," said Sarah-Jane. "And very Educational."

The End